the VERY WORST ever

Catch ZOO LaTeR

BY ANDY NONAMUS
ILLUSTRATED BY AMY JINDRA

LITTLE SIMON

NEW YORK LONDON TORONTO SYDNEY NEW DELHI

This book is a work of fiction. Any references to historical events, real people, or real places are used fictitiously. Other names, characters, places, and events are products of the author's imagination, and any resemblance to actual events or places or persons, living or dead, is entirely coincidental.

LITTLE SIMON

An imprint of Simon & Schuster Children's Publishing Division

1230 Avenue of the Americas, New York, New York 10020

First Little Simon paperback edition May 2024

Copyright © 2024 by Simon & Schuster, LLC

Also available in a Little Simon hardcover edition.

All rights reserved, including the right of reproduction in whole or in part in any form.

LITTLE SIMON is a registered trademark of Simon & Schuster, LLC, and associated colophon is a trademark of Simon & Schuster, LLC.

Simon & Schuster: Celebrating 100 Years of Publishing in 2024

For information about special discounts for bulk purchases, please contact Simon & Schuster Special Sales at 1-866-506-1949 or business@simonandschuster.com.

The Simon & Schuster Speakers Bureau can bring authors to your live event. For more information or to book an event contact the Simon & Schuster Speakers Bureau at 1-866-248-3049 or visit our website at www.simonspeakers.com.

Text by Matthew J. Gilbert

Designed by Hannah Frece

The text of this book was set in Causten Round.

Manufactured in the United States of America 0424 LAK

10 9 8 7 6 5 4 3 2 1

Library of Congress Cataloging-in-Publication Data

Names: Nonamus, Andy, author. | Jindra, Amy, illustrator.

Title: Catch zoo later / by Andy Nonamus illustrated by Amy Jindra.

Description: First Little Simon edition. | New York : Little Simon, 2024. | Series: The very worst ever; book 3 | Audience: Ages 5–9. | Summary: A class field trip to the zoo takes a chaotic turn when a creep of geckos accidentally escapes.

Identifiers: LCCN 2023048472 (print) | LCCN 2023048473 (ebook) | ISBN 9781665954631 (paperback) | ISBN 9781665954648 (hardcover) | ISBN 9781665954655 (ebook)

Subjects: CYAC: School field trips—Fiction. | Schools—Fiction. | Zoos—Fiction. | Humorous stories. | BISAC: JUVENILE FICTION / Humorous Stories | JUVENILE FICTION / Readers / Chapter Books | LCGFT: Humorous fiction.

Classification: LCC PZ7.1.N6378 Cat 2024 (print) | LCC PZ7.1.N6378 (ebook) | DDC [Fic]—dc23

LC record available at https://lccn.loc.gov/2023048472

LC ebook record available at https://lccn.loc.gov/2023048473

CONTENTS

Hey, Reader!

Thanks for checking out my story. Though I gotta warn you, I can't ever let you know my real name or what I look like. This may seem weird, but trust me, it's very important that I stay a secret.

Why? To protect myself! Seriously, these stories are super embarrassing!

Plus, you might even know me already! I could be in your class, on your baseball team, in your ballet class, or playing the tuba in your school band . . . anywhere!

Hi!

For all you know I could be sitting next to you right now!

So I went ahead and scratched out my name and put a sticker on my face, so you don't have to. You're welcome.

Now, we can both enjoy reading all about my awkward life . . . if you're into that kind of thing.

Peace out!

PERMISSION SLIP SLIP-UP

Have you ever had one of those days where you wake up and everything is just right?

Usually, my days are a messy blur of running late, spilling sticky breakfast all over me, or accidentally wearing two different shoes.

But today? It was nothing like that.

Today, I arrived at school *extra* early. I was *extra* excited. Everything was *extra* perfect. This was because today was ... FIELD TRIP DAY!

It was like the weekend traded places with a weekday, bringing my friends along for the fun!

Outside the school building, my class gathered at the school's bus zone. Kids chatted excitedly, dressed in their field-trip best.

Jake Gold, all-star athlete and all-star best friend, was doing something strange with his knees. This was called "exercising."

FWEEET!

My other friend, Regina du Lar, coached him with her tablet. She tapped it and a sound came out like a coach's whistle. *FWEEET*!

"Time out!" she shouted, then smiled at me. "Look, Jake, ▮▮▮▮▮▮▮ is here!"

"Ninety-eight ... ninety-nine ... one hundred!" Jake counted out loud. He paused his jumping jacks and smiled. "Hey, bro! Don't mind me. I'm just prepping to be the fastest thing at the zoo today."

That's where we were going today— the zoo. And it seemed like Jake was ready to race whatever he found in there.

"Good luck with that," I said, then
realized we were missing someone.
"Huh. Where's Glinda?"

"Right here," Regina replied, taking
a step to the side.

Glinda Alegre, the final member of the group, stood behind Regina. Instead of her usual clothing, she wore a loose outfit with skulls on it.

I raised my eyebrows. "Is Glinda wearing . . . pajamas?"

"Yes, she's still sleeping," Regina explained. "When Glinda's having a really good nightmare, she would rather stay in it."

"How is that possible?" I asked, waving my hand in front of Glinda's sleeping face. "And who has good nightmares?"

Glinda let out a long snore.

"Line up, class!" a voice suddenly called.

It was our teacher, Mr. Hughes, standing by a bus door. He wore an elephant hat, with large ears on either side of his head. "You know the drill. I need signed permission slips before you take your seat on the Zoo Express!"

"It's just a bus," the driver called from his seat.

"A *Zoo Express* bus," Mr. Hughes corrected.

Kids opened their backpacks and pulled out their signed slips. This was my cue to get mine. I dug around and found an old cookie, loose pencils, and basically *everything but* a signed piece of paper.

Just where was that slip?

"Come on, ▓▓▓▓▓!" Regina called, filing onto the bus with everyone else.

Oh no. I started to panic.

My slip was nowhere to be found. I felt like I was suddenly spiraling into a nightmare of my own. And not a "good" kind like Glinda's.

VROOM-VROOM RESCUE

VROOM!

The bus's engine roared to life. I was the only kid left standing outside.

Mr. Hughes frowned at me. "All good over there, ████████?"

"Um, just one second!" I said, digging around even in my pockets. Maybe I shoved the paper in there!

Will the bus leave without me? Will my friends have fun with someone else? Some kid who actually has a permission slip?

VROOM-VROOM! the bus roared again.

Only it wasn't the bus. It was something else buzzing up the street. *Fast.*

Suddenly, a motorcycle came flying through the air. Its wheels sailed over our heads before it swerved into a stop next to me. The mystery biker took her helmet off and smiled.

"Mom!" I said with relief. "What are you doing here? Don't you have a new job at the motorcycle repair shop?"

My mom had new jobs about every other week. That was the cool thing about her—she could do anything!

"I sure do, but you left this at home," she said, passing me a piece of paper. It was my signed permission slip!

I was so happy, I jumped on her for a hug. But I remembered a mom-hug in public is a serious no-no. So I stepped back quickly. (She would get a longer hug later at home.)

"Oh, and you also left this!" She pulled out a teddy bear. It was dressed in a doctor's coat. "Dr. Cuddles!"

Blushing, I looked up and saw a few kids and the bus driver snickering.

"Mom!" I groaned as I stuffed Dr. Cuddles into my backpack. "You know he likes staying warm in bed!"

Normally, the entire grade finding out about my secret teddy bear would ruin my day. But not today. Not when I had the Zoo Express to hop on.

I handed the permission slip to Mr. Hughes. "Here you go! One mom-delivered slip, hot off the motorcycle grill!"

He took it and stepped aside. "Welcome aboard!"

Skipping inside, I found my friends
sitting all the way in the back.

Jake patted the empty spot beside
him. "Saved you a seat!"

"Thanks!" I said, sliding in.

Regina and Glinda sat on the opposite side of the aisle. Well, Regina sat while Glinda still snoozed on. She really was an odd one.

SNORE

Mr. Hughes clapped his hands together, getting everyone's attention. "Are we ready to head out, class?"

"YES!" we shouted.

"And are we ready to sing the whole way there?" he asked, lifting a tiny flute.

"NO!" everyone shouted.

"Okay then!" Mr. Hughes slipped the flute into his coat pocket. "Guess I brought this for nothing."

The bus driver sighed. "Let's hit the road already."

3

BUS GAMES

You know what's nearly as exciting as a field trip?

The bus ride *to* the place you're visiting.

There are all sorts of fun games to play on the bus. There's one called Scream When You See a Cow.

Basically, you shout about cows.

Or so I've heard. Our town didn't really have many farms, which meant we didn't have many cows. So, we shouted about dogs riding in cars instead.

"Poodle in a red sports car!" a kid called out.

"Growling Chihuahuas!" another kid announced. "In that pink van!"

A third kid yelled, "There's a beagle driving a truck!"

Everyone rushed to my side of the bus to see, smushing my face against the glass.

"Oof!" I said.

Everyone oohed and aahed, but all I could see was my own foggy breath. I blinked really fast so my eyelashes could clear it up.

"False alarm," Regina said, using her tablet camera to zoom in on the truck. "It's just someone who *looks* like a beagle."

"Awww!" everyone groaned as they slumped in their seats.

Mr. Hughes grabbed his flute. "Don't fret, kids! I'll sing about the beagle!"

"NOOO!" we shouted. (The bus driver did too.)

Mr. Hughes ignored us. *"The beagle in the truck goes WOOF, WOOF, WOOF! ALL THROUGH THE TOWN!"*

"Who cares about dogs?" Jake scoffed beside me. "You're all missing these amazing ANTS. I see ants on billboards and even on bicycles! It's a giant ant invasion!"

He was looking through a pair of binoculars. Naturally, they made everything seem way bigger than it actually was. With a sigh, I took the binoculars away from his face.

"*Now* what do you see?" I asked.

"Ohhh," he said. "It's a *tiny* ant invasion!"

Just then Mr. Hughes burst into another song. *"The wheels on the bus are AT THE ZOO, AT THE ZOO, AT THE ZOO! Look, everyone, we're at the zoo! Who's ready to go?"*

As I turned to look out my window, the kids from the other side of the bus

rushed over to get the best view of the zoo's entrance. Again, my face was smooshed against the window.

But I didn't mind. I couldn't wait to see what happened next on this field trip! I just needed to unstick my face from the glass first.

A CLASS-Y VACATION

We were welcomed with balloons and a guy in a lion suit holding a sign. It read LET'S GET "ZOO" IT, STUDENTS!

In a place filled with cool animals, it felt like *we* were the main attraction.

"Ah! The red-carpet treatment," Regina said, snapping a selfie with the lion guy.

See, her family was super famous for their video game company. They did fancy red-carpet events all the time.

Jake did a handstand, inspecting the ground. "Red carpet? Regina, this is concrete."

I helped tow the sleeping Glinda along to receive our special student visitor wristbands. I slid mine on with a smile.

"A whole day with no schoolwork!" I cheered. "It's almost too good to be true."

"Because it is," Mr. Hughes said, approaching us with one hand behind his back.

I raised an eyebrow. "Are you about to feed us to whatever you're hiding behind your back?"

"The only thing I'll be feeding is . . . YOUR MINDS!" he said.

He revealed what he was holding. It was a giant stack of worksheets. He passed them out to everyone.

"'Roaring Awesome Field Trip Questions,'" Regina said, reading from the paper.

The class groaned.

"But I thought field trips were like a vacation from class!" someone said.

"More like a *classy* vacation!" Mr. Hughes said. "Get it? Classy? Like . . . it's still class-y?"

For the first time ever, Glinda and I had the same looks of gloom.

"As you visit the different exhibits, fill out these worksheets and learn all about the animal kingdom!" he said. "Questions?"

Jake raised his hand high. "Me! Over here! Sir! Pick me!"

Mr. Hughes sighed. "Yes, Mr. Gold?"

"Is there a prize for finishing first?" Jake asked, jumping in place. "Like a trophy? Or better yet, RACING A CHEETAH?!"

"Ahhh, no," Mr. Hughes said.

Everyone booed. But then he dug something out of his pocket. It looked like an old chocolate wrapped in gold foil.

Mr. Hughes held up the dusty old candy. The kind of old candy you just can't eat. "But if you write down extra fun facts, you can win *this*. It's deliciously sugar-free."

Jake pumped his fist with excitement. "Woo-hoo!"

The whole grade cheered—except me. Of course, my group would ask for extra work to win a prize I couldn't eat. *Just my luck.*

DINOS AT
THE ZOO

You'd think our zoo would be just like any other, but my jaw nearly hit the floor when I looked at the map.

The list of animal exhibits went on *forever*.

There was Bear Barn, Lion Lane, Bat Cave, Hippo Hangout, Monkey Manor, and even Zebra Zone.

The list was as long as the jungle's longest snake!

(Okay, not really, but it was still long.)

"This is the biggest zoo in the country," Regina said. "Did you know one of our Du Lar video games is set in the crocodile feeding area?"

I gulped. "Crocodile *feeding* area?"

"She means the Croc Cafe," Jake said. "It's totally awesome. But first, you gotta see the dinosaurs."

Did he say ... *dinosaurs*?

In a green, leafy exhibit, I could hear something coming at me full speed. Something huge. Something hungry.

"The dinosaur is coming," Jake whispered.

My knees locked. My eyes shut. I waited to be swallowed up whole. But instead, all I felt was a warm, wet tongue wrapping around me.

I opened my eyes and saw a giraffe!

It lifted me off the ground with a friendly lick of its black-blue tongue. At this height, I could see a sign on the ceiling that read FREE GIRAFFE BATHS!

Guests around me clapped as the giraffe set me back down. It left gobs of spit all over me.

Jake looked in awe. "I thought dinosaurs didn't exist anymore. But here they are."

"Giraffes aren't ... oh, never mind." I wiped slobber off my face.

Regina pointed. "Look, ▮▮▮▮▮▮, you're on the giraffe cam!"

I looked up to see my horrified face on a bunch of TVs all around the exhibit.

"Great," I sighed. "I'm a famous human lollipop."

Regina started filling out her worksheet. "Okay, our first Roaring Awesome fact is . . . giraffes can pick things up with their tongues!"

We filled out ours too, and I helped Glinda with hers. She snored in two bursts that sounded like "Thank you."

After visiting the giraffes, we chilled with the polar bears. Then we flapped our arms and tried to fly at the Bird Breakaway enclosure. We even ran back and forth in front of the dolphins at the Sea Sanctuary.

For our next stop, I suggested the Butterfly Wing. But Regina ran toward a dark, mysterious cave with a glass door.

"I just love this place!" she said. "Come on, guys!"

As my friends trickled in, I read the sign above the door.

REPTILE REALM, it said.

A chill rushed up my spine. At least, I hoped it was a chill.

6

GREMLINS BE HERE!

The door slowly closed behind me. *CREEEEEEAK.*

At first I couldn't see a thing. But my eyes slowly found the low-lit tanks with beady little eyes in them. *Lots* of little eyes.

"It's just us in here!" Jake shouted, his voice echoing.

"Shhh!" I said.

What creepy-crawlies were hiding here, watching us? The thought gave me goose bumps. There was only one cure for my fear—Dr. Cuddles.

In the dark, I quietly dug him out of my backpack and hugged him tight. It's not like my friends would see him. I was so wrong.

Dr. Cuddles's white coat glowed in the dark like a furry spotlight.

"Interesting light," Regina said. "It's very cute!"

"Don't you mean *beary* cute?" Glinda hissed, suddenly standing beside me.

I yelped. "I thought you were sleeping!"

"Who says I'm awake?" she replied with a snore. "Now, follow me...."

Not sure whether she was awake or still in dreamland, we followed Glinda

down a narrow tunnel. A glowing sign read YOU'RE ENTERING THE SCALY REALM . . . SHHH. GECKOS, ALLIGATORS, AND CRITTERS BE HERE!

Okay . . . that wasn't creepy at all.

In one tank, I saw a slithering tail.

In another, five pair of eyes winked at me.

"She's leading us out to the food court, right?" I asked, hopeful.

"No," Glinda said. "I'm leading you to ... DRAGONS!"

"Dragons?!" Jake cheered. "Maybe they'll want to wrestle."

I somehow tripped over my own two feet and tumbled right into the wall. A pair of eyes blinked down at me from a tank above. The thing was green and scaly. It was even sticking its tongue out at me!

"DRAGON!" I screamed, crawling back.

"It's only a *bearded* dragon." Regina laughed and pointed to an information card below the tank. "'Like a chameleon, the bearded dragon changes colors.'"

The bearded dragon looked at me and suddenly changed to a blue color.

It walked away, looking bored.

(It changed colors, while I needed to change underpants.)

"What a Roaring Awesome fact," I said shakily. "Let's add it to the worksheet and go!"

"Wait!" Jake said from a nearby tank. "Look at these tiny crocodiles."

Jake was actually looking at something called gremlin geckos. I was too afraid to look, so I just read their information card.

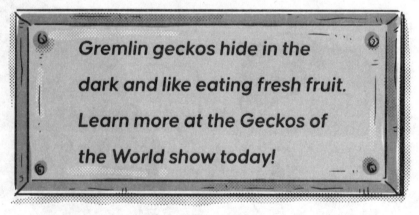

Gremlin geckos hide in the dark and like eating fresh fruit. Learn more at the Geckos of the World show today!

I wasn't interested in the geckos, no matter what world they came from.

"What kind of glass is this?" Regina

peered into their tank. "My family's been working on a new screen for gaming tablets. This one might work! Let's get a closer look."

She grabbed Dr. Cuddles, using him like a flashlight. "Hmmm, this isn't bright enough. Maybe I can use my mini light. . . ."

Regina pulled out a device with all sorts of buttons. She tried holding the bear, the device, her worksheet, and pencil, but nearly dropped everything.

"I'll help," I said. Anything to get us out of here faster.

I meant to grab Dr. Cuddles but as luck would have it, my clumsy fingers accidentally pressed a button on her device instead. It made a few beeping sounds, then attached itself to the gecko's tank with a loud *POP*!

It whirred, it crackled, and then . . .

HISSSSSSSSSSSSSS.

I whispered, "What . . . is . . . *that?*"

7

CRAWLING FREE

Regina frantically tried to turn the device off. "Why would you push the unlock-everything button?!"

"Why do you have something with an unlock-everything button?!" I asked.

We watched as giant bolts came unscrewed on the geckos' tank.

Like a scene from a scary movie, all we could do was watch as the tank slowly opened.

I finally got a good look at them. They were scaly geckos with many teeth and glowing yellow eyes. They even had little bumps on their bodies that looked like thorns. They scurried onto the floor, hissing at us like snapping turtles. One stood still and screamed for no reason! There were hundreds!

(Okay, it was more like twelve or thirteen.)

Doing what any other kid would do in this situation, I tried to save my teddy bear. "Go, Dr. Cuddles! Save yourself!"

I threw him down the tunnel, hoping he'd go through the exit doors. Instead, he sailed right into the garbage can.

(Note to self: learn how to throw.)

"This is fun," Jake said, chasing after the geckos. "It's like playing with scary puppies!"

He backflipped into action. But the little critters were faster than him, zipping through his legs. Jake ran in circles, nearly smacking his head on the cave wall.

"I don't suppose that device has a catch-everything button?" I asked Regina, hopping from foot to foot.

"Very funny!" she said, reaching for one of the geckos. It tail-swiped her hand away and ran over her shoes.

The geckos ran toward the exit door, where Glinda stood sleepily with wide-open arms. If the geckos wanted to escape, they'd have to get through her first.

"Glinda!" I shouted. "You're our only hope!"

But when they reached her, Glinda simply opened the doors and let the geckos escape.

"Be free, my scaly friends!" Glinda cackled evilly.

And with that, a dozen or so reptiles vanished into the zoo.

"We'll never win Mr. Hughes's pocket chocolate now," Jake groaned.

Regina paced back and forth. "Okay, let's think. The gecko show won't start for another hour. How many geckos were there? Eleven, twelve? I bet we can find them all."

"Something like that," I said, still not sure how many I'd seen.

Regina reached into her backpack. "We'll need a little help from my friend here."

She pulled out a drone.

8

DRONE IT OFF!

We flew into action!

Well, the drone did. We ran after it as Regina soared it over the zoo exhibits.

On the screen, Regina could pilot the drone *and* see what it saw. It felt as if we were flying with birds. The drone loop-the-looped.

Regina helped it dodge poop as it
flew. Sadly, she couldn't help the guy
eating an ice-cream cone.

KA-POOP!

He had bird poop all over his
delicious treat.

"More bird poop incoming!" Jake
warned.

"Poop . . ." Glinda snored on Jake's
back. "Gross . . ."

Watching Regina fly the drone

through the zoo was so fun, I nearly forgot our mission. We had to find all the gremlin geckos. So far, we had zero.

Jake moved his eyebrows up and down, over and over.

"What are you doing?" I asked.

"Flexing my brain so I can think better," he explained. "Okay, what did that little card say about the geckos?"

"It said they like the dark," I recalled. "And fresh fruit."

Jake snapped his fingers. "Okay! So they have to be in dark places and wherever they sell fruit."

Whoa. That was a great point!

We flew through the food court. Luckily, the first thing we saw was a snack cart called Wild about Fruits! It had every fruit imaginable, but no geckos.

Then, I noticed something odd in the berry basket. Two of the fresh strawberries were squirming around.

I pointed at the screen. "Critter alert!"

It was two gremlin geckos, snacking away. They let out a squeak at the drone and scurried out of the cart.

"On it!" Regina said, tapping fast. The words VACUUM MODE flashed on the screen.

With that, the drone vacuumed the critters up safely into a net.

"Two down, ten more to go," Regina counted.

Or eleven? I thought.

Glinda, still sleeping, said, "Bats . . . bats . . . bats . . ."

Regina snapped her fingers. "Good thinking, Glinda! Bats like the dark AND they like eating fruit. Come on!"

In the Bat Cave, we didn't even have to spend too much time searching.

Three of them fell right into our laps. Bats air-dropped them right to us from above their tank. They squeaked in annoyance as the geckos ate away at a papaya. My guess? The little monsters had taken their snacks.

"Thanks, scary birds!" Jake said to them.

We found four more geckos relaxing on a leaf floating in the Hippo Hangout lake. They were so content, they barely noticed the drone scooping them right up!

"Three more to go!" Jake cheered.

"Or four," I said. "Go, team!"

Regina suddenly gasped. "Wait. Where's Glinda?"

Jake pointed ahead. "She's over there!"

I spotted Glinda sleep-marching back to the Reptile Realm. Behind her, two geckos followed along as if they were hypnotized.

"We'd better move fast," I said. "Before Glinda leads them out of the zoo."

9

TAIL ON, TAIL OFF

We burst into the Reptile Realm.

Glinda was curled up on the cave floor with her geckos. They were both fast asleep, nested in her hair. It would've been kinda cute . . . if the geckos weren't so creepy.

Carefully, I plucked the sleeping geckos from her hair.

Then the drone whizzed by and gently plopped the geckos it had into the tank too. Next it beeped off and fell into Regina's backpack.

"That makes eleven," Regina counted. "We're only missing one."

"Or two!" I reminded her.

But no one seemed to hear me. The drill sounded on Regina's device as she bolted the tank back into place. Just as she finished, a voice called out, "Hey!"

It was a zoo worker. He said, "The line for the gecko show is *outside* the cave. No cuts!"

"Look," Regina whispered to me. "His hat."

At first, I didn't notice it ... but now it was clear as day. The final gecko was sitting on top of the worker's hat. This one had sharper spikes and looked bigger than the others.

"It's the boss gecko," I whispered back. "We need to trap it."

"Hey, should I challenge him to a push-up contest?" Jake whispered.

"You know I can hear you, right?" the worker said. "And you don't need to worry. This is Hector!"

Casually, the zoo worker took the gecko right off his head and into his cupped hands.

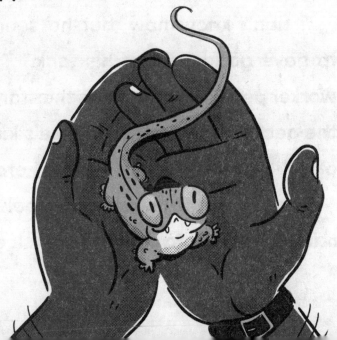

"Hector?" we echoed.

"I don't know how, but he seems to have gotten out of his tank." The worker petted Hector. "He's the star of the gecko show today. See, he's kind of a full-*scale* celebrity around here."

Jake, Regina, and I shared a look of relief. Even Glinda smiled in her sleep.

No one knew we'd set the geckos free. The worker thought Hector had somehow escaped all on his own. We were in the clear!

"Do you want to hold him?" the worked asked, passing me Hector.

"Oh, uh . . . sure," I said.

Cupped in my hands, Hector looked at me with suspicious eyes.

"He likes you," Regina said as she snapped a picture.

"Yeah . . . ," I said, smiling. "He's actually kind of cute! One time, my mom bought me some gecko-shaped gummies. I thought I was eating real geckos!"

Hector did not like this. As I went to pet him, he must've thought I was going to eat him like a gummy. He squeaked and then his tail dropped ... right ... off.

10

NUMBER THIRTEEN

"Bro!" Jake screamed. "You broke that gecko!"

In one hand, I held Hector. In the other, I lifted the snapped-off tail in horror. I carefully held the tail between my two fingers.

I looked back and forth between my friends and the tail.

The gecko narrowed his eyes with a look that said, *"How. Could. You?"*

"B-but . . . how?!" I cried out. "Can we glue this back on? Did this happen because I accidentally set the geckos free? Oh please, zoo worker! Don't send me to zoo detention!"

The zoo worker frowned. "Wait—
you set the geckos free?"

Glinda snored, suddenly beside me.
"Get it together, ███████. It'll grow
back on its own."

Regina, Jake, and I said, "Huh?!"

"The weird sleeping girl is right," the zoo worker said. "Geckos drop their tails when they're spooked or surprised. But they can grow back. He probably thought you were going to eat him like a gummy!"

As I stared at the tail with my jaw dropped, the worker patted my back. "You're from the field trip class, right? They're heading over now. Why don't you show off what you've learned?"

"Maybe it'll be worth extra credit," Regina offered.

Jake rubbed his hands together. "Mr. Hughes's old pocket chocolate is as good as ours!"

Believe it or not, the gecko show was a total success. And it was thanks to me!

After I shared my unlucky story with the class, I earned a lucky amount of extra credit for my group. I showed Mr. Hughes the gecko tail. He seemed impressed . . . and a little concerned.

"Maybe we should all stick together next time," he said.

As we filed onto the bus at the end of the day, there was still something I couldn't get out of my mind.

"Regina...," I started.

"Yes?" she asked.

"Are you sure there were only twelve geckos we set loose?" I asked. "For some reason, I really thought there was one more."

"Not this again," Regina said. "There were only twelve. Now, stop worrying. Let's fill out the final question of our worksheet."

I looked at my paper and read it. *What's the most surprising thing you learned today?*

Already knowing my answers, I wrote them down:

WHAT I LEARNED

Glinda is a sleepy genius.

Regina is the best flyer

at the zoo. Her gizmos are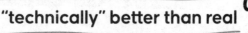

"technically" better than real

birds.

Jake has a sweet spot for

helping his friends . . . and

a sweet tooth for expired

chocolate.

And me? I survived the

field trip and had a tale to

tell about a dropped tail.

Rm.# : 312   Name:

When I was finished, I thought I felt something wiggling on my back. I reached and tried to feel around, but there was nothing there.

How strange!

Climbing into the bus, I tried to enjoy the ride home. I was sure there wasn't anything to worry about.

HERE'S A PEEK AT
_____'S
NEXT
ADVENTURE!

How well do you remember your dreams?

Some kids are Duhhh-reamers.

These are kids who can't remember their dreams at all. When they try to remember a single detail, they go: "Uhhh…"

An excerpt from *Happy Gift Day to You*

Other kids are Dream Weavers.

Now, these kids dream up some silly things. Sometimes they're knights flying on the backs of giant chickens. Or maybe they float all the way to outer space for an alien-filled picnic.

But me? I just dream about things like screaming vultures.

I'll explain.

In my dream this morning, I skipped through a meadow with birds. It was like those movies where the animals sing with a princess. But I wasn't dressed like a princess. Instead, I wore a top hat and a duck floatie.

An excerpt from *Happy Gift Day to You*

Why? Because it was a dream! Everything was just peachy...

...until the inflatable duck turned into an ugly, screaming vulture.

"You are forgetting something IMPORTANT!" the vulture screeched. *"WAAAKE UUUP!"*

"AHHH!" I screamed. "Go back to being a cute duck!"

But the dream vulture wasn't listening to me. *"WAAAKE UP! WAAAKE UP! WAAA–!"*

I jumped awake. On the nightstand, my alarm clock rang loudly.

An excerpt from *Happy Gift Day to You*